The Treasure Hunt

by
Llinos Mair

Wenfro

O! Gwyn ein byd
– a gwyrdd!

Pont

'Who wants to come on a treasure hunt?' asked Mam-gu Iet-wen. It was a fine autumn morning and the sun was shining.

'We're ready, Mam-gu Iet-wen!' shouted Owen and Olwen.
'Ho, ho...off you go! I'll keep an eye on you from here,'
croaked Branwen, the white crow who could see
everything through her Wen-Cam.

Save water!

'What kind of treasure will it be?' asked Olwen.
'Aha! It won't be just one treasure. You're going to find many treasures,' said Mam-gu Iet-wen with a smile.

Bwgi-bo the scarecrow came to find out what was going on.

Bwgi-bo the scarecrow always thought a lot but he never said a word.

Peeking out of Bwgi-bo's pocket was Prydwen the spider.
She felt excited too.

So, Olwen, Owen, Bwgi-bo and Prydwen went on a treasure hunt with Mam-gu Iet-wen.

First of all they saw Glanwen the sheep, who was busy spinning wool in the field.

'Well done Glanwen,' said Mam-gu Iet-wen. 'I'll come over tomorrow to help you dye the wool a lovely colour. Then you can knit me a nice warm jumper.'

As they crossed the field, Bwgi-bo made his way over to the pond, clinking and clanking noisily. There was a grumpy frog sitting on a leaf.

'There aren't many tasty bugs to eat as winter draws nearer - so we might as well go to bed,' said a sleepy toad nearby.

The toad looked hungrily at Prydwen. He thought a spider would be a tasty snack! But she was safe in Bwgi-bo's pocket.

Good night!

Mam-gu Iet-wen found lovely ripe rosehips in the hedge nearby and she began to gather them. Olwen went to help her.

Just be careful! The thorns on thi. rose are prickly.

Owen pointed to a prickly brown creature shuffling through the leaves.

Without waiting for anyone to answer, the hedgehog rolled himself into a ball and was fast asleep in no time.

'He will sleep right through the winter too,' said Mam-gu Iet-wen.

Because his tummy's full of bugs like me!

'Our tortoise loves to sleep as well,' thought Owen.
'Many animals hibernate, all snug and warm until spring,'
added Mam-gu Iet-wen.

High above them in the hedgerow there was a cluster of hazelnuts.

But Mam-gu Iet-wen was not the only one to spot them...

A flash of red fur and a bushy tail went streaking by, with an armful of nuts to store for winter.

'Well, that squirrel has plenty of food to tuck into!' laughed Prydwen.

They all crossed the field and followed the path up to the rocks nearby. Owen peered into the dark cave.

'Ssssh...' said Mam-gu Iet-wen. 'No, but there's someone else sleeping here. Someone very small, and black as night.'

Suddenly, Owen spotted another creature. Rolled into a coil by the rock was a green snake.

The snake opened one eye, gave Olwen a very friendly wink,
and went back to sleep.

'Blackberries! Are these the treasures?' cried Olwen, surprised. This wasn't what she was expecting at all.

It must be a trick.

'Don't sound so disappointed, Olwen fach. Have you ever seen such big, juicy ones? They're delicious,' said Mam-gu Iet-wen. 'They're the treasures of the hedgerow.'

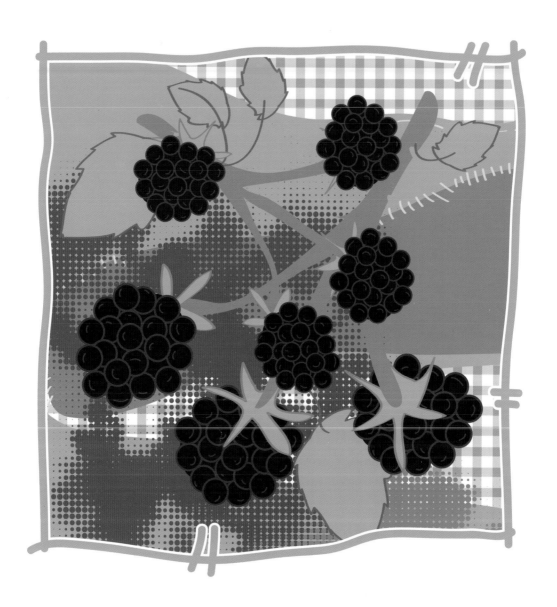

They gathered the blackberries until their fingers were purple and their bowl was full to the brim.

In the bowl, some of the berries were squashed and rotten. Bwgi-bo was turning up his nose at them.

'No, Bwgi-bo. They're for Glanwen, for dyeing the wool,' explained Mam-gu Iet-wen. 'Blackberry juice will make a lovely colour.' She was keen to have a new purple jumper to keep her warm in the winter.

Olwen was very quiet as they made their way home. She wasn't sure if the blackberries were real treasures.

Of course they are Olwen! And it was you who gave me the idea for them, you know. Remember when you brought an expensive packet of blackberries from the supermarket? It made me think of all the treasures we have here where we live.

Overseas Produce
£3.00

And she gave her grand-daughter a big cwtsh. Olwen felt happy.

Owen was very excited about helping Mam-gu Iet-wen in the kitchen.

'Yes, there will be enough treasures here for us all,' said Mam-gu Iet-wen.

Bwgi-bo was very happy with his treasure.

Jingle-jingle! Clink-clink! He danced and shook his body all the way home to Iet-wen.

The treasure hunters were all very tired after their long walk.

For Ffion Haf – our little treasure! x

First published in 2015 by Gomer Press, Llandysul, Ceredigion, SA44 4JL
www.gomer.co.uk

ISBN 978 1 84851 858 2
ISBN 978 1 84851 926 8 (ePUB)
ISBN 978 1 84851 938 1 (Kindle)

Sponsored by the Welsh Government.

Printed and bound in Wales by Gomer Press, Llandysul, Ceredigion, SA44 4JL